# To Tom and Shirley, with a son's love.

Library of Congress Cataloging-in-Publication Data • Names: Fenske, Jonathan, author.
Title: Plankton is pushy / by Jonathan Fenske. • Description: First edition. | New York, NY : Scholastic Press, 2017.
Summary: Plankton tries hard to get Mister Mussel to return a friendly greeting, but when Mussel finally opens
his mouth the results are unfortunate for Plankton. • Identifiers: LCCN 2016026077 | ISBN 9781338098969
(paper over board) • Subjects: LCSH: Plankton—Juvenile fiction. | Mussels—Juvenile fiction. | Courtesy—Juvenile
fiction. • CYAC: Plankton—Fiction. | Mussels—Fiction. | Etiquette—Fiction. • Classification: LCC PZ7.F34843 Pl 2017
DDC [E]—dc23 LC record available at https://lccn.loc. gov/2016026077

10 9 8 7 6 5 4 3 2 1        17 18 19 20 21
Printed in Malaysia    108
First edition, May 2017
Book design by Steve Ponzo

# Plankton Is PUSHY

Jonathan Fenske

Scholastic Press · New York

When I say "Hello" …

… you say "Hello."

"Hello."

Perhaps I should slow it down just a wee bit?

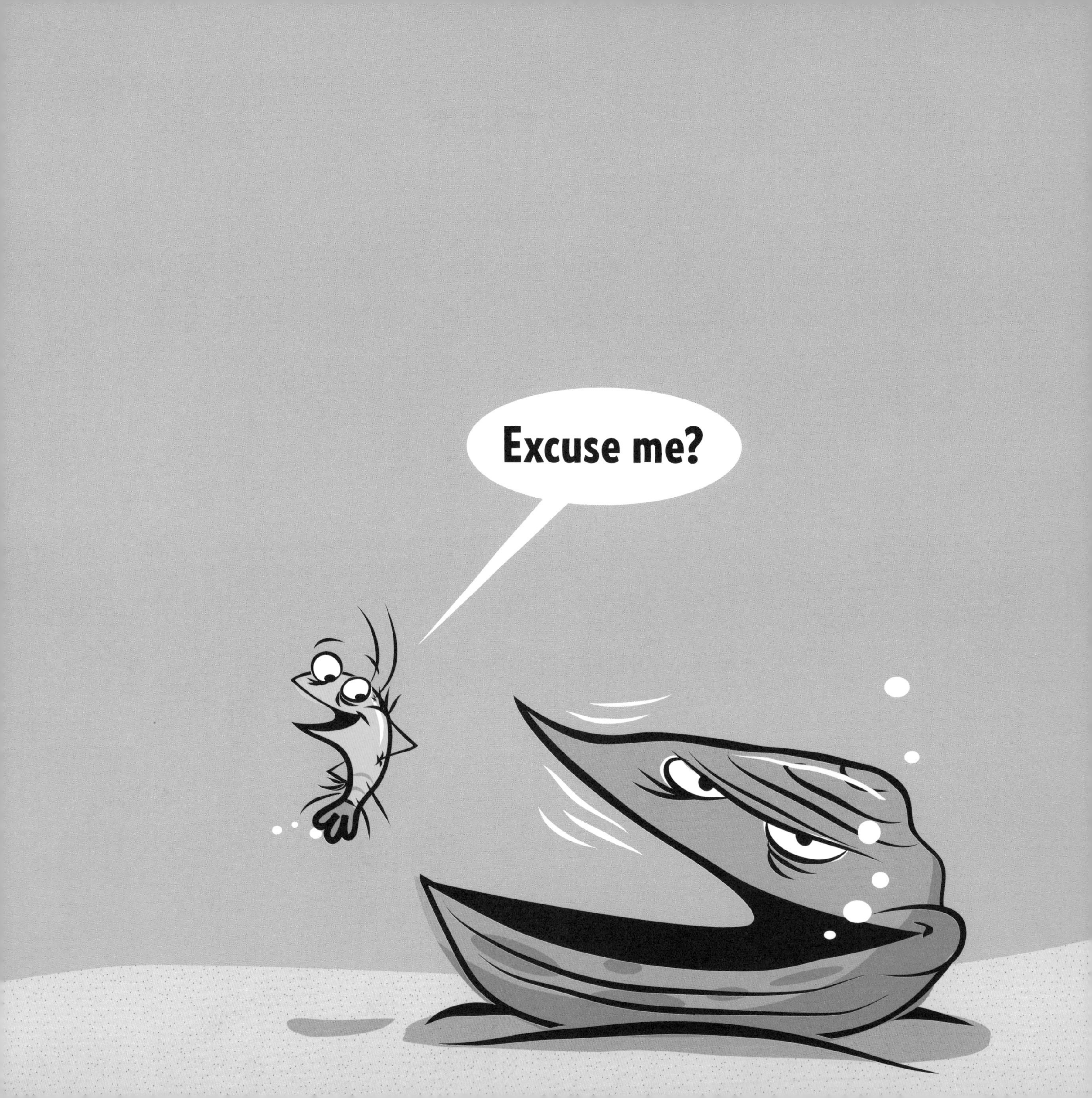
Excuse me?

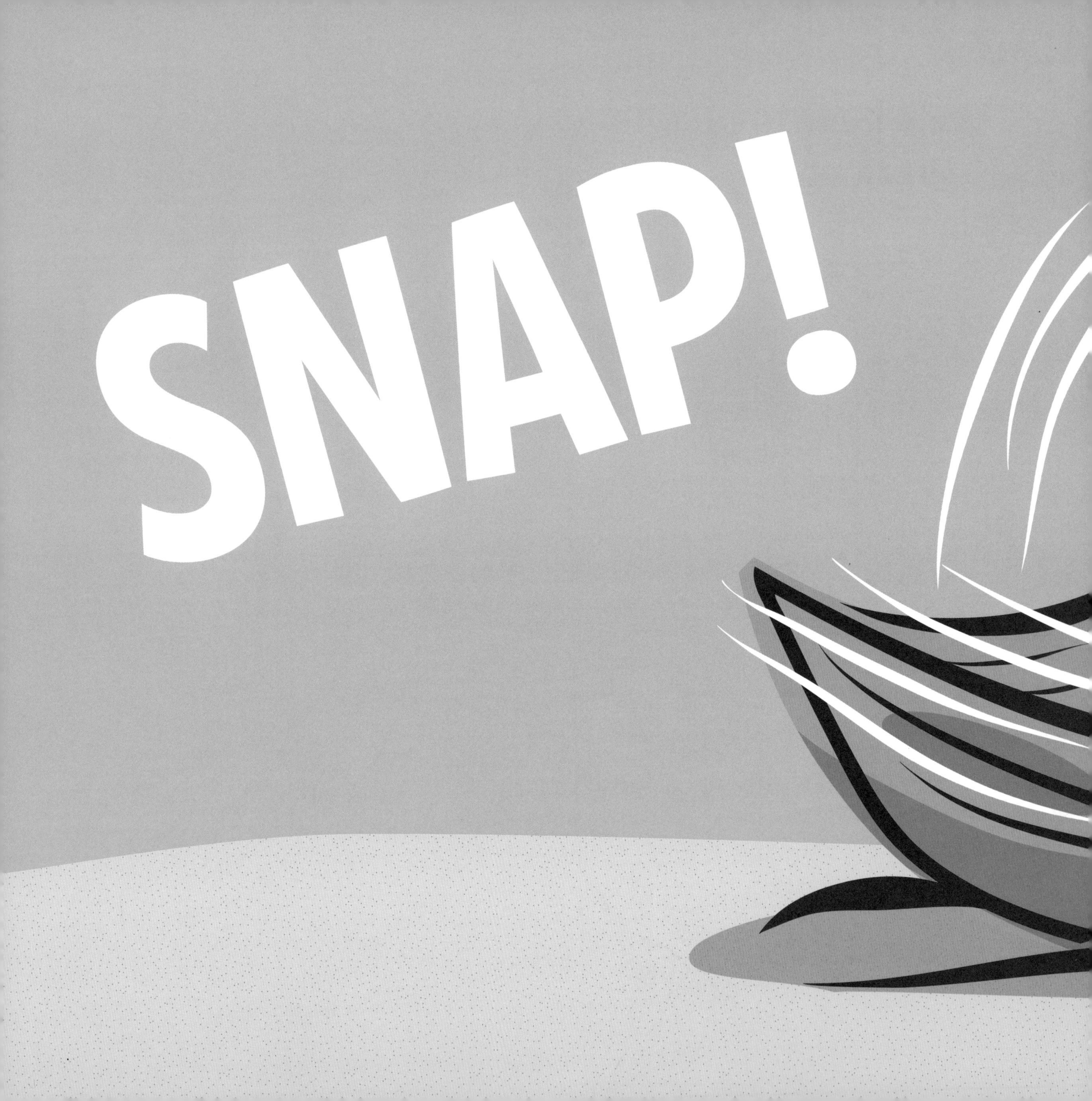
SNAP!

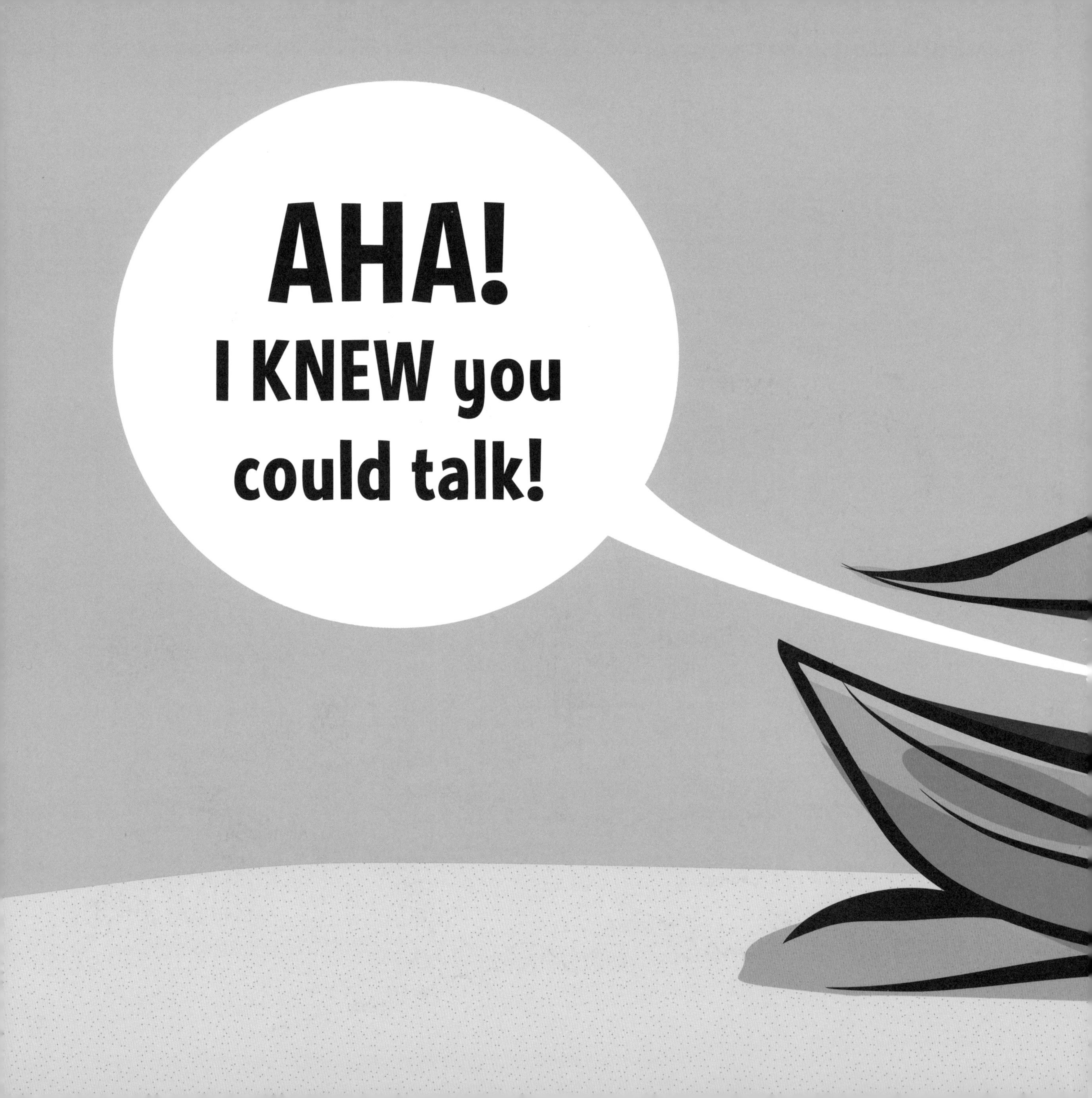
AHA!
I KNEW you could talk!